THE UNKNOWN PATH

THE UNKNOWN PATH

ALEXANDRU CRISTIAN

THE UNKNOWN PATH

iUniverse books may be ordered through booksellers or by contacting:

iUniverse
1663 Liberty Drive
Bloomington, IN 47403
www.iuniverse.com
844-349-9409

Because of the dynamic nature of the Internet, any web addresses or links contained in this book may have changed since publication and may no longer be valid. The views expressed in this work are solely those of the author and do not necessarily reflect the views of the publisher, and the publisher hereby disclaims any responsibility for them.

Any people depicted in stock imagery provided by Getty Images are models, and such images are being used for illustrative purposes only. Certain stock imagery © Getty Images.

ISBN: 978-1-6632-3124-6 (sc)
ISBN: 978-1-6632-3123-9 (e)

Library of Congress Control Number: 2022905712

Print information available on the last page.

iUniverse rev. date: 03/25/2022

"Our duty in the face of a true mystery is not to clarify it, but to deepen it so much that we change it into an even bigger mystery."
Lucian Blaga

David drops his pen on the floor. Tired, he is leaning on the file. An enormous weight tightens his shoulders bending him. It's the hardest job he's got to accomplish. He has been planning for at least a year to retire, but the prospect of a household life scares him. He's going to risk it for the last time. He has to; this is the life he got used to: running, madness, existential chaos. He never started a family, and he doesn't have a stable relationship with the woman he loves. He is an everlasting explorer, a seeker in the waters, mountains, valleys, tunnels, in all the innermost recesses of the earth.

The phone rouses him from his musing.

"Hi, I called you ...," a calm and quiet voice says.

"I know why you called me! You need me."

"You are so modest!"

"You have to admit that I feel you need me. Please, what is it?"

"I have a very difficult case that I have to solve. I have an almost impossible mission."

"I see. When can we see each other?"

"In twenty minutes I'll come to the café that we both know."

"Good."

"Thanks."

He turns off the mobile, and a sense of shame floods his entire body. He's ashamed of Nick. He's always helped David, and he almost never returns the favor. Why couldn't David intervene when he was detained because of some nonsense caused by others? Why didn't he help Nick when he was hospitalized, even though he had a doctor girlfriend? A tiring "why" is stirring up his mind.

He stands up fast, puts on a dark green shirt and dark pants, and quickly goes to the café. Outside it's sunny, with a feeling of tranquility that he has always hated. He sees Nick sitting outside and looking through the café window.

"Hey, I'm here. Stop looking inside."

"I was looking for an intimate place where we could talk."

They enter the café and find a semi-obscure purple lit place on the right side. They sit down and order a large cup of coffee.

"You look tired and upset," Nick says. "What is bothering you?"

"Nick, I have an infernal case to solve. You came without a phone, I guess."

"Get straight to the point."

"I was hired for a very large sum," David says, "by a rich and eccentric man."

"All the rich are eccentric."

"Yes, but he was also an important man in the Intelligence Service, and I suspect he has ties to several discreet societies, as I call them. I was thinking that such a man would be more sensible or more balanced. That man lives in an indescribable fantasy. He hired writers, doctors, and teachers to help him discover all the mysteries of history and of earthly life."

"So you need to find out something too."

"All right, Nick. I need to know the ultimate truth about the true leadership of the world."

Nick's broad smile freezes David. "And did you say yes?"

"Of course I did. At first I found it fascinating, but now it's awfully hard. I have to find out this pyramid, but I'm afraid I'm going to disturb forces that I can no longer master."

"Have you set up a strategy?"

"Frankly, I'm kind of baffled."

"Well, then go home, and for a week research all the secret or discreet organizations you've heard about. Then you come to me, and we compare them. I was in charge of something like that a long time ago."

"Thanks a lot, Nick, I promise I'll try."

"Let's go now because you have a whole week of work ahead."

The two men greet each other respectfully and leave the café separately. David is thinking about what's coming. Nick's trying to throw out a thought that came back to his mind.

He opens his computer and sits comfortable on the chair. He gets a pen and a sheet of paper. He searches the net for hours, but he doesn't find anything else except for ordinary secret organizations. His list is divided into secular and sacred organizations.

Secular organizations are the World Business Club, World Economic Club, Planetary Industrial Group, Money Organization, Pildrun Group, Bolenberg Group, Infinite Blue Order, Group of Twelve, and Group of Twenty. Clerical organizations are the Order of the Holy Chair, the Order of the Cross and Sword, the Organization of Salvation of Mankind, Katharsis, the Order of Genesis, and the Black Order of the Sacred Seat. He's discovered a new legendary society, the Group of the Thirteen Judges. He circles it with a bright color and decides to get more information.

He rewrites this list, which is not very long, on a parchment sheet and underlines a few features for each. There are common features known by anyone who navigates on the information superhighway. The main purposes of such societies and organizations are world governance, a single economy, a world government, a unique race, a unique religion, the end of war, and a global village. The millenary traits don't bring anything new. They're all in the same spirit.

He emails a friend, Vick, who's an organization and conspiracy expert. He attaches the list and asks his friend to add some more names. After he finishes eating a sandwich, he calls up Nick.

"Hi, I found a few things and I made a general list. But I'm still working on it."

"Okay. When you think you're ready, you come to me, and we'll discuss it. I'll help you indulge him."

"Okay. Thanks a lot."

He opens *yahoo mail* and sends the list to the billionaire, who signs all his emails as *Money*, and tells him that he will continue his research. Then he lies on the couch to rest. After some time the phone awakens him from the numbness.

"Hello."

"What are you doing? Why didn't you call me back?" It's Amy.

"Hi, honey, I had a lot of work."

"I don't believe you. You met another woman."

"That's not true, but you know, I told you I have one last job to solve."

"You're a liar. You've been doing the same thing for years. You're lying with no shame. You're some no-good who doesn't want to have a normal life."

"Forgive me, but one day you will understand the whole situation."

The empty sound of the receiver makes him realize that no one is listening to him. He loves Amy in his own way, but he can't tell her everything. He's not allowed to. His mentor in the detective profession told him that everything he knows must only be known to him. Not even his shadow is allowed to know it, and by this he meant his physical shade, not the queues sent by the intelligence services.

He opens the email and notices a message from Vick.

Hi, I saw the list. But you missed a lot of them. Intelligence Services, influence groups, lobbies. I corrected it a little bit. I noticed you asked about the Group of the Thirteen Judges; I found out something, but there's a missing link that I don't understand. What specific interest links the Intelligence Services with the Group of the Thirteen Judges and the World Business Club?

Why am I telling you this? All the heads of important secret services are members of these groups—for example, Phill Longham from the Intelligence Agency, Frédéric Bayeux from the Intelligence Service, Moshe Haaretz from the Intelligence Institute, Will Sloane from the Intelligence Directorate, Gerhard Schimmwell from the Federal Security and Counter-Intelligence Service, and Yuri Banuţki from the External Intelligence Service. And something else which is very important: everyone is allowed access to the London City and the Pontifical Library. So we have got something, but we don't know exactly what. I guess the power chain looks like this.

1. The World Business Club is closely linked to the Group of the Thirteen Judges.
2. The Intelligence Services have a close connection to these groups.
3. The Vatican and London City are aware of these groups.
4. Another organization that unites and patronizes them all is missing, because, as we know from history, the occult societies and the world are ruled in a pyramidal way.

David, I'll get back to you with any further information I may find. Print this page and delete the email at once.

Keep in touch, Vick.

David sits back in the armchair and smiles. *I found a good lead, but I have to find more somewhere. I'm going to the Vatican. I have to take this step or else find someone from there.*

With his eyes closed, he thinks of his experience as a young detective, of the missions he accomplished for the service that recruited him, and then of his private career. All his mentors advised him to retire when he wanted a family and felt he could no longer work well. He turns off the computer, gets dressed, and goes jogging in the park. Hard days wait for him, and physical conditioning should not fall behind.

David's phone rings, but he ignores it, dozing off again. Later he answers the phone, sleepy.

"What are you doing? You scared me! I thought something had happened to you."

"No, I slept very well and for a long time. What's on your mind?"

"Let's meet at the café."

"Okay, I'm coming."

He dresses in whatever he can reach and quickly heads downstairs and out to the meeting place. Nick is waiting for him, looking extremely serious. David smiles and hugs him.

Nick leads him inside and they sit. "Let's talk."

"What news do you have?"

"Please give up this case."

"Why?"

"I have information that the man who made you do these things is a traitor."

"What do you mean?"

"This Money, as you call him, is an international cheat. He has bankrupted two banks, the Murray Bank in Scotland and the Bank of Zeit in Germany. He is officially a refugee in Switzerland, but he is actually on Mustique Island in the West Indies where he has a luxury estate. He is officially a shareholder in a Swedish investment fund.

"Money, birth name Sergei Alexandrovich Mill, is a second-rate Russian aristocrat born out of the wedlock relationship of a Russian countess with a Scottish adventurer. Due to his mother's position and his father's relations, he grew up in Switzerland, attended the Monte Carlo High School and the Faculty of Psychology of Canterbury University in England.

"He entered Masonry at the age of twenty-five, reached the thirty-third degree, and was kicked out after scamming several organizations and humanitarian foundations. His latest great deception was to bankrupt the Foundation for Helping the Poor of the World; he got three billion dollars. His accounts in Switzerland are now estimated at ten billion, and his Cyprus account amounts to 1.5 billion euros. He was a Russian spy and an Israeli spy and betrayed both countries. He attempted to enter the Black Order of the Sacred Seat, but he was rejected by a conclave of ten cardinals."

"Nick, you are amazing. How did you find out everything?"

"You don't have to know how. I just want to warn you. How much money did he give you?"

"Two million euros at the opening of the case, and on its closure he is committed to transfer me ten million in an account in a tax haven—this is what Money told me."

"Lots of money. And what exactly did he ask you?"

"What the pyramid of the world looks like and who precisely leads the world."

"And why does he want to know that?"

"He told me he had a plan and that he needed to know this."

"Interesting, so it looks like this gentleman is playing doubles."

"What are you talking about?"

"He wants to find out the pyramid of world Freemasonry and use money to corrupt people in its leadership."

"What must be done?"

"Pretend you're doing your job, and I'm going to consult someone."

"All right, we're talking."

"Keep in touch."

Nick gets up and leaves abruptly; David orders a whiskey and sinks into thought. His whole life has been a struggle to learn secrets, and now he's the main character of such a story. How interesting life is!

IV

He gets home and turns on his computer. He checks his email inbox and notices nothing interesting; no more illogical emails. He picks up the phone and calls Money.

"Sir, I want to see you and talk."

"Hi, David, I'm afraid I'm in Geneva. I'll send someone to pick up the information for me."

"Can I at least send you some new information by email?"

"Of course, but please send it to me on the private address. You seem worried; what's happened?"

"I'll explain in the email."

He heads toward his desk, but suddenly hears a short knock at the door. When he opens it, in front of him stands a middle-aged man who hands an envelope to him.

"Sir, this envelope is from Mr. Money; you'll find all your tasks inside. Mr. Money is upset; he knows you've been doing research about him. Please stop it because you will only end up in a room without escape."

David takes the envelope and looks at the man, who turns and slowly walks away along the hallway. David goes to the couch and feels that things are getting complicated. There is a small photo album inside the envelope. The pictures show Money in Switzerland with his wife and children, then in Paris. Next to the photos is written a short message: *David, this is me. Please stop researching.*

He throws down the file, agitated, and leaves the house. He walks down the deserted streets, thinking he has to do something with his life, to get out of this vicious circle. He must put an end to these missions that are destroying him. He goes to the street where Amy lives and watches her house for hours. He doesn't want to lie to her, but she can't understand that he is a research man, a shadow man. This thought will frighten her and will make her stay away from him.

He doesn't have the guts to get closer to her house. He goes to the nearest terrace, orders a coke, and thinks he needs a change. He calls Vick, who does not answer. He goes to the municipal library to look for a book, but can't find it.

On his way home he is stopped by a young man in an old-fashioned outfit. "David, please give up Money's case. You've annoyed someone very badly."

"Who are you? How do you know—?" Before he finishes asking, the man has run away.

Scared, he heads home quickly. He goes inside, blocks the windows, and bolts the door. He makes a large cup of tea and turns on his computer. The inbox has two important messages from Vick and Nick.

The email from Nick is brief and straight to the point:

> David, stop the research. You're being chased by an extremely powerful organization that won't hesitate to **kill** you. You don't have to know its name. If you continue, an assassination order will be issued, and it will be carried out by the Order of the Shadows, namely professional assassins. Can

you understand? Stop the searches, and run away from Money and the rest of them.

PS: Vick knows a lot because he's involved.

David reads this email in amazement. "Vick is my lifelong friend," he says aloud. "I don't believe he could do anything like that. This is an invention of Nick's to protect me. However, let's read Vick's email ...."

David, I have new information.

The Group of the Thirteen Judges oversees three extremely secret orders consisting of people who have officially been declared dead under various circumstances. The first one is the Order of the Shadows, a strong order consisting of former spies trained to kill. It is ruled by a supreme killer, who in turn is one of the thirteen judges. The second order is the Order of the Tunnel, in charge of establishing a large international espionage network. It is led by a supreme chief who is also one of the thirteen judges. And the final order is the Order of Souls, a semi-legendary organization supposedly ruled by a forever cursed soul, Rotham the Black. Rotham is the thirteenth judge, and he is part of a council of three eternal wise men, considered the strongest people on Earth in all of history.

Subordination to the Group of the Thirteen Judges is purely symbolic and has esoteric aspects. Many people challenge the existence of this group and associate it with the Luciferian-Satanic guidance sects. The purpose of this order is to conquer souls for hell and to promote pleasures and sins in the world. I don't know the other Satanic orders, but I know they are led by the other two eternal wise men. According to some data, the names of these orders are the Order of the Black Blood and the Order of the Archangel of Hell, led as the legend says by the cursed souls of the Knights of Darkness, the wizards Gahael and Elihaim. In conclusion, the three eternal wise men are Rotham the Black, Gahael, and Elihaim, all the rulers of evil.

I'll be back with more information. Now we have almost every organizational chart of the world; I'm going to send it to you in a few days. But there's another organization I need to know more about. It is the organization that controls the others, and it is a bridge between the two worlds.

David suddenly turns off the computer and starts writing all the information. He's not going to take anything for granted from now on. He'll start working on the case and send it to Money as soon as possible. *I have to get rid of Money and his entire story.*

The phone vibrates in his pocket, and he takes a look at the screen: an unknown number. He answers, somewhat scared.

"David Baldoni?"

"Yes, it's him speaking."

"Hi, I'm Abraham Watson, and I want to see you as soon as possible. I have new information about what you're interested in."

"Okay, I'll give you my address, and you come to my place."

"I agree."

Half an hour later the doorbell rings. He opens the door and gawks in surprise. It's the young man who warned him in the street.

"Abraham."

"Nice to meet you, David. I'll get straight to the point. You're in great danger. Thanks to your interventions, I found out that your computer was used to send important data to the Pentagon."

"What do you mean?"

"We have this information from Nick; he told us you're a double agent—Israeli and Russian. And from your computer, data was sent to the Pentagon, which the latter considered dangerous. To be more specific, you obtained data from the Pentagon that you sent to the other intelligence services, and then through an error you sent it to the Pentagon. That's how it got out. You and I will have to delete all this information from your computer. Otherwise you will be arrested and sentenced to death for high treason."

"Yes, but I'm not on American soil."

"Right, but you're an American citizen, and you know I can find and arrest you."

"Okay, what do I have to do?"

"Delete all data from your computer in front of me. To make your task easier, I brought a device that will help you delete everything in less than an hour."

David turns on the computer and introduces the device that will destroy his work of a lifetime. All the cases solved, all his private detective work. Luckily he has them all saved on a few memory sticks stored in a safe deposit box at a bank in Switzerland.

"I'm sorry it reached this point, but we were forced to. You know too much. And this Money thing is not good for you at all."

"What should I tell Money?"

"Tell him your computer broke down and you lost everything."

"Fine, if you say so. But the man gave me money."

"You give it back, I guess you haven't spent the whole amount."

David looks in the void as the data is slowly being deleted. Why did Nick betray him? Would Vick be involved? Or does Nick actually protect him? He hates betraying and lying and has had it around his entire life. The questions continue to pour through his mind in a dizzying waterfall.

Tired of all these thoughts, David gets up and lights a cigarette, blowing the smoke at Watson. "You got what you wanted. Now you can go."

"Believe me, I've done everything for you. Nick asked me to protect you with the price of my life."

"Thank you, though I don't think so."

Abraham Watson rises and leaves, and David is consumed with the desire to forget everything. Forget about Money, Nick, Vick, and secret organizations. He just wants to sleep—and then to see Amy and start a new life.

He goes to bed and soon falls deeply asleep. Outside the window next to him, large drops of lazy rain stretch, and the clouds take forms resembling occult effigies.

V

The strident sound of the microwave oven awakens him to reality. A large cup of coffee in his hand, he looks glumly toward the gray sky with golden spots letting sunlight through. He thinks of the bitter destiny of Judas Iscariot.

Why are there treason and lies everywhere? He doesn't think Vick betrayed him, but he's terrified at the thought that his lifelong friend Nick betrayed him. They started working as detectives together. Nick went to the Agency, while David turned to private business. He established a company he led for ten years. He collaborated with Nick on all his important projects. He found the economics teacher's lost daughter, discovered a two-hundred-year-old manuscript, recovered a bank account in the Cayman Islands. His job brought him great prestige. He was considered by many as one of the world's most important detectives.

He met Vick when he worked on finding old manuscripts. Vick is an independent researcher, an encyclopedia of esoteric, conspiracy, and metaphysical theories. He was an ardent collaborator with the Agency.

He looks at the computer and decides to turn it on. He doesn't know why, but something attracts him to this file. There are too many question marks. The inbox shows no email; he looks in the spam folder and sees an email from Vick titled "Evrika"—that is, "I succeeded." It opens, and David hesitantly reads it.

Hi, David, I hope you are sitting down and comfortable. Please make sure no one else sees this email, so make sure you DELETE it after reading and writing down EVERYTHING!!

I found the world leadership pyramid, and I send it to you attached to this email, and I also discovered a diagram of planetary domination. I confess that we are close to finding who holds the gilded chains by which the world is being enslaved.

Your honest friend, Vick.

Restless, he looks at the attachment, rises from the desk, lights a fruity cigar, and looks into his coffee mug. He's going to give Vick one last chance. Why is he thinking about this file? Why is everything so fascinating? It's just the fantasy of a crook, full of money and vanity. He clicks Download and reads carefully.

The world is ruled by the three eternal wise men. These three are cursed souls from hell, assimilated to demons. Their names are Rotham the Black, Gahael, and Elihaim. Rotham the Black is the one who manipulates people and stimulates their desire for money and gold; Gahael is the one who possesses them with the erotic impulse, and Elihaim is an archicon, that is, a demon who is a theologian and cheats people with false religion. The archicon is a demon of reason.

These three are empowered by the powers of evil to destroy the world and the legacy of Christ. What I want to point out is that this leadership is legendary and attributed to metaphysical forces. The battle between good and evil takes place for the souls of humanity. Jesus Christ Himself said, *"I Am not the ruler of this age."* As you know, the apocalypse is a revelation of many mysteries.

With respect to the actual leadership of the world, it is ensured by the Group of the Thirteen Judges. The first twelve judges are the most influential people in the world, each in his field, including the two heads of the Orders of the Shadow and the Tunnel. The last, the thirteenth, is considered to be Rotham the Black, who reigns over humanity by the power he holds on money. He is one of the three eternal wise men. The rest of the organizations are subordinated to this group.

I'm sending to you a pyramid of world power on another page along with an interesting diagram of how the world can be mastered.

In the first case of the pyramid I decided to type the initials of the semi-legendary rulers of this age. David, I repeat that this is a diagram I drew on my own initiative. I did not refer to the supreme power assigned to God nor to the power attributed to Lucifer.

But I have an important question. All these organizations and societies have the same goals. Even if they are led by a narrow circle, there must be something that harmonizes their objectives. That is why they consider that the scheme lacks the actual organization that truly leads the destiny of this world, as well as the path of history.

I hope all this information is useful to you.

RGE 3

Group of 13 Judges

The World Business Club
The World Economic Group
The Planetary Industrial Group

Katharsis, Genesis Order, The Order of the Cross and Sword
Secret Services and Deep and
Low Profile Organizations

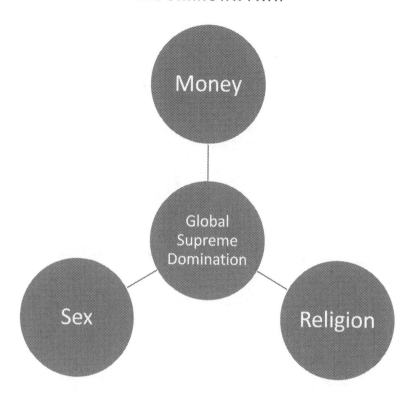

Abruptly David closes the email tab. He copies everything and picks up his phone. He calls Nick, who doesn't answer. He then calls a long-forgotten number, the number of his mentor in the Agency. After five rings, he hears a loud voice on the phone.

"Hi, David, how are you?"

"Fine, I'm busy. I want to see you as soon as possible."

"Of course; let's see: tomorrow I pass by your city and I can meet you at your place."

"I'd rather see you in the park and talk quietly."

"I understand, without other inquisitive eyes around us. Well, then—see you tomorrow at four or five o'clock in the afternoon, okay?"

"I'll be there, Wilson."

"Good."

He lets out a relieved breath. He hasn't been in touch with Wilson for five years. He was David's instructor at the Agency; he taught him everything he knows. Now Wilson has retired to a farm and is a prosperous businessman. He's got his own dairy factory.

David tries again to call Nick but only gets a busy signal. So he sends a short email to Vick: "Thank you so much. You're a reliable friend. Yours, David."

Then he calls Amy and establishes that he will meet her tonight. He wants to spend his time with the woman he loves and who cannot know the terrible situation he is going through. The wind strikes slowly in the window, while the branches dance as in a Shostakovich waltz.

VI

The next day, after a night with Amy such as he hasn't shared in a long time, he's getting ready to meet Wilson. He explained to Amy that she couldn't come with him, and she kicked him out in a real fit of jealousy. He stops at the café next to the park and drinks a warm tea. His gaze falls on a black car with a government number plate. He smiles; this reminds him of long periods of time with Wilson when they were trailing one target or another.

The waiter comes and lays a newspaper on his table; relaxed, he looks through the society news, the same turbulent politics, and the news about famous people. But on the inside back page he reads something that freezes his heart: "Famous scientist killed in a car accident. The well-known conspiracy theory researcher Paul W. Morowitz died on his way home in a road accident, after a truck entered the wrong lane. The truck driver said he had fallen asleep while driving."

His phone rings, and he responds absently.

"Hi, I'm here, I'm waiting for you at the fountain in the park. Hurry up; otherwise all the kids are going to believe that Santa Claus came to town."

"Wait, Wilson, I'm on my way. Listen, I read something—"

"Shut up and come quickly."

He sets out for the park, and instead of taking him two minutes, the walk takes more like five. When he arrives, he sees Wilson wearing a big cowboy hat, a bushy white beard, and cheerful green eyes.

"You have changed so much …?"

"I told you everybody would confuse me with Santa. How are you doing, man?" He stands and hugs David strongly.

"Okay, I was appalled. I'm working on a controversial case, and I read something terrifying."

"Okay, pull yourself together and say it."

"Morowitz was killed last night, and I'm working to find out something about a conspiracy theory."

"What? Did everyone's exposer die?"

"I wonder why."

"He must have found something. Tell me all about yourself."

"I work for an eccentric billionaire that some people consider a big crook; he goes by the name of Money. He hired me to find out whether or not there is a world government or a potential world leadership. Yesterday I received an extraordinary long and explicit email from Vick about this government. I found out about the Group of the Thirteen Judges and the three eternal wise men."

"Buddy, you simply don't want to be a good boy! Do you want to get in trouble like old Morowitz? You found out enough. Go and give all the information to that Money or whatever you name him, and stop it."

"Is there anything else to find out?"

"Yes, there is a lot more, but you don't need to know. I found out a few things, but I'm afraid to talk. There is a secret organization, some kind of assassin's order, and if they find out that you know a lot about any society they protect, they eliminate you. The matter is extremely serious. Remember how Willie disappeared. He went home, and nobody has heard a thing about him for seven years. I just know he had found out about this group you're telling me about, the Thirteen or Twelve. I don't know how many they are, and I don't care."

"Yes, I know what you're talking about, it's called the Order of Shadows, consisting of assassins who protect all the esoteric and metaphysical secrets."

"But why did you have to get into this mess? I thought you were going to stop, and you wanted to end it with all the dangerous, stupid things. I've known you retired for over five years, but now I can see, you did not start your quiet life."

"I know what you're saying, Wilson. You know, I'm terribly sorry. I found a good and honest girl, and I want to stay with her, but I don't know how to get out of this."

"Here's the plan. I shall come over and have a drink, and you'll show me everything you know. Then we do the file together and send it to Money."

"All right, come on."

"Let's take a ride around the town. I haven't seen the downtown for a long time."

"Come on, Wilson."

As they're both walking toward the center of town, they notice a black car following them slowly; it looks like the one David saw earlier. Wilson takes his arm and directs them toward a narrow, winding street. Then he enters a shopping mall, pretending he wants to look for a new pair of shoes.

VII

Vick turns on the light and surveys the mess he left around him. He lives in a modest apartment full of papers and documents. He works in parallel on two books about the true meaning of world history. An advocate of the theories that history is directed, Vick tries to find out what the true destiny of the world is and how it has been influenced.

He stares at the Morowitz news on the internet and calls Nick, who's not answering. He stops reading and goes to lie down. After a few minutes of rest, he hears a loud noise at the door. He rises, frightened, and looks through the peephole. The corridor is empty, but a paper has been left on the floor. He quickly opens the door, picks up the paper, and makes sure the door is secure. He crosses the room to look out the window and doesn't notice anything, except for a deserted street where a noise lost in the night may still represent a little sign of life.

He looks at the paper and goes very still.

Stop all investigations now and avoid sharing
the fate of others who searched the wrong place.
Better not to know than be a dead man who
knows everything. Nick.

What does Nick have to do with this case? How does Nick know what he found out? And what the hell is he trying to tell him?

He phones Nick again, but still there's no answer. Then he turns on the computer and writes an email to David. After finishing, he writes out all the information he holds, seals it in a green envelope, and leaves it on the table. He's found what he was looking for, but he didn't have the guts to say. David's going to know everything. But the question remains: what has Nick to do in this matter?

He looks at the clock and goes to bed, He needs sleep and time for thinking.

He can't fall asleep, as he is thinking that Nick still knows something. He gets up and calls David, but he doesn't answer. Then he decides to call the priest, the only one he trusts.

After many rings, he responds. "Vick, you scared me. What has happened?"

"Nick found out everything, and I have to protect David."

"What do you mean, because I don't understand anything?"

"The Group knows about his existence."

The voice of the priest becomes silent. His breath turns into a strained whistling. The priest knows everything Vick has been doing.

"And how exactly did they find out?"

"I don't know, Father, but they found out."

"I'll think about it till tomorrow."

"I've made up my mind. I'm going to send you an envelope and a letter from me for David, and I'll be leaving for good in another country."

"What are you afraid of?"

"That … that Nick is one of them."

"Does David know?"

"That's not exactly why I'm afraid for him."

"Okay, tomorrow I'll stop by your place and then go over to him. Go get some rest now."

"Thanks, Father, you're a real friend."

Vick's looking at the phone that's beeping in the void. He takes a pen and writes a few lines for David, then looks at the envelope and smiles bitterly. He rises and goes to his safe. He dials the code, removes all the money from it, packs it up, grabs a glass of wine, and looks out the window. He'll leave no matter what happens. David will know the truth. As a matter of fact, there will be two of them, he and the priest.

VIII

avid and Wilson get into the house, cheerful. They sit on the couch, drink a glass of wine, and tell stories. They talk about their lives, their loves, and their fame, about the Agency, and about the fate of some others. At some point the phone rings. David notices Vick's number but does not respond and continues to feel very well, a state of mind he has not had for some time, in the company of his mentor and friend. Vick can wait until tomorrow.

"Wilson, you know what I want to find out about?"

"Of course I do. You want to know a world that you should not be interested in. It is a world governed by some powers that have no relevance to us."

"I want to close the case; the man did give me a lot of money. Then I want to live a quiet life with Amy."

"That's how I want you. Hey, how's Nick doing?"

"Nick's a traitor. He sent someone to delete all the data in my computer under the pretext that he wanted to protect me, even though he lied to the Pentagon, saying I'm a double agent or I don't know what nonsense."

"I can't believe it. You two were like brothers. In fact you do not know …."

"What?"

"Nick is involved in the thing about Willie's disappearance, I'm sure."

"Why do you say that?"

"Because he suddenly sent him on vacation. But at the same time I know he didn't approve him taking the plane and sent him by car instead. From what I heard, Willie was burned alive on an isolated road leading to a bunker."

"That's terrible, but what did he find out?"

"That there is an organization that runs the world and has all the world's power in its hands."

"Well, what is that?"

"It was not known because Willie's car, which was full of papers, was taken by the Agency and caused to disappear. The boss gave me orders not to try to find out what happened. And shortly after, he promoted Nick."

"It's obvious. But how did he find out?"

"I don't know this. I just know that you have to get out of this thing. It's a necessity for you, it's like oxygen. I want you to stay alive, David."

"I know, Wilson, but I promised the man."

David goes to the computer to turn it on and reads some news on the internet. Then one news item freezes his blood. Billionaire Sergei Alexandrovich Mill has had a heart attack in Switzerland and is hospitalized in Geneva in serious condition.

"Really, Money wasn't lying; he sent me the pictures. And now what the hell am I doing?"

"Relax. Let's work on the file. You put in two or three pieces of information from Vick, then you send it to Money's address, and you can consider yourself reconciled."

Just then the phone rings; it's Nick. Scared, David responds, giving Wilson a sign to stay quiet. "Hi, Nick."

"Hey, you heard about Money. See how good life can be on the island? Tell me, are you completing the mission or not?"

"I'll send the information to you."

"Please give me an email with everything you know. Maybe I can help you with something."

"Absolutely."

"Let's talk tomorrow; sleep tight."

"Thanks, you too." David closes the phone and swears. "What a colossal nerve!"

"Nick is extremely sure of himself because he knows he can find out everything."

"Wilson, please tell me, who does Nick work for?"

"He still works for the Agency; that's all I know."

"Please tell me the whole truth."

"Okay, I'll tell you, though I don't think it's a hundred percent true. Nick is the head of the liaison division with foreign secret services and has great influence and a high rank in the Agency. This position has allowed him to enter several more or less occult power circles. He also runs a mixed interventions brigade—that is, special operations with various objectives. What I do know is that Nick is part of an extremely select group from which there are a number of important people of the world's intelligence services."

"But what you're telling me is quite interesting. I didn't think Nick was that strong."

"I still know that a few years are missing from his résumé. I know he's gone to a few countries, but there's no telling what he did out there."

David stares into the distance, thinking bitterly about Nick. He cannot be the traitor to the Agency.

Wilson looks around David's desk and says, "David, let's set to work and send the envelope with all the information by tomorrow. Money will be grateful to us."

They both sit at the computer and start working on the "Planet" file, David's last file before his final withdrawal. While writing, he notices how the phone is illuminated continuously. It may be Amy. *I'm sorry, but this job will be over soon.*

IX

After the morning service the priest leaves, almost running from the church. He's heading to David's house. He rings at the door, and David opens after a short time.

"Hello, Father. What's the matter?"

"I have an extremely important message for you from Vick and an envelope with confidential contents."

"But what happened to Vick?"

"He completed the task and decided to leave the country forever. But he left all the information to you."

"Thank you, Father," David answers in a listless voice. *What happened to Vick? He must have found something terrible.*

David turns abruptly at Wilson's voice, raised in terror from the computer. "David, come quickly!"

"What happened?"

"Read what it says on the web."

David looks and almost faints. The priest catches him so he doesn't fall on the glass table behind the desk.

The father reads, and a state of confusion penetrates his mind: "A veteran of the Agency, Nicholas Page, was found drowned in the river on the outskirts of the city. Military prosecutors suspect a suicide. They confirm the presence of important documents in Page's briefcase. We'll be back with new information."

The two of them help David lie on the couch. After some time David wakes up with a terrible headache. Next to him, the priest is carefully guarding him.

"Where's Wilson?"

"He left urgently for the Agency to find out something about what happened."

"I feel so tired. I want to check my email; maybe I have something new."

"I suggest you rest. I'll make you a soothing tea, and then you sleep a little."

"Okay, Father, whatever you say."

After drinking the tea, David grows visibly drowsy. The priest browses through all the documents and is stunned. How much could Vick know? Too much for a mere researcher …. A voice interrupts his musing.

"Father, I feel better."

"David, you lie down until tomorrow, and we'll take stock then. Tell me what I can do."

"I've mostly finished the Wilson file. Please send it to the post office."

"Okay, but which file is it?"

"There's a yellow one on the table, full of paperwork and schematics. It's for the eccentric who paid me to get in this gutter."

"Well, there's none out there."

"There's no way, it was there when I found out the terrible news."

"Do you think Wilson left with it?"

"I don't believe that he needed such a file."

"Maybe he needs information for the Agency."

"Wilson's been out of the Agency for more than ten years."

"Or he needs information for what you're looking for."

"Father, how can a farmer need something like that?"

"David, you forget that such people retire feet first. Even a poor priest like me knows it; someone like you should all the more."

"I can't believe it," David says, slapping his head. "Wilson's into this file. That's why he immediately agreed to come and help me. That's why he accused Nick of helping Willie disappear."

"David, I read what Vick wrote here. I think Wilson is part of a group or order that deals with exactly what you hate."

"What?"

"Attaining world supremacy."

avid's gaze rises vaguely over the priest's silhouette. A faint light flickers' it's the electronic clock. In these moments David wishes to forget everything and to be gone once and for all from this place and from this time. He barely notices the priest letting himself out.

After a few days David awakens from lethargy. He has just sat in bed and thought about how to get out of this complicated situation. Is Wilson the traitor, or is it Nick? Vick knows something more, and that's why he's gone.

He rises and goes to the computer. He opens it and his eyes hurt him. He realizes that he has spent more than two days in total darkness, and his eyes cannot bear the weakest light. The mail box shows him a single message. Feeling sick, he opens it. It's from Money.

Hello, David. I'm better. I'm at a clinic near Geneva now. In a few days I will go to Saint Moritz, and from there I will return to work. If you complete the task, you can send the folder to the address that I have attached to your mail. As far as I'm concerned, for now I want to take care of myself and my health. Once you send me the file, I'll send all your money to your account. I only have to wish you a quiet life from now on.

Best wishes and thanks for everything, Money.

After reading the message, he looks around for the file, but it seems to be missing. He rises and searches every nook and cubbyhole. Under the bed he discovers a large green envelope that says "Vick." He opens it up and notes dozens of pages and hundreds of schemes about what he's been looking for. He grabs and retrieves some of the information. By the end of the day he will complete the task; then he will put everything in the post and end this career.

The phone calls—an overseas number. He answers.

"Hi, David, it's Abraham Watson. Give me your email address."

"Why?"

"To redeem my mistake, I will send you everything you deleted from your computer."

David recites his email address. "What happened to Nick?"

"I'd rather not talk about this topic on the phone. I'm sending it to you now."

"Okay, thank you."

After he hangs up, he turns on the TV and watches a movie. He has forgotten to relax for a long time. His thoughts fly to the life he's going to have with Amy. He's determined to stay with her all his life. He'll do the right thing and stay with her. This is his destiny. In the window the sun drops toward the horizon, throwing its last rays over the green envelope.

A doorbell wakes him from lethargy. He goes and opens it without checking through the peephole. Amy enters quickly and jumps into his arms. They kiss each other long, then go to the bedroom. There he will tell her everything he knows and what plans he has for her.

XI

On a nice tidy lawn Money looks at a tree. He remembers the trees of his own childhood. He is reading a poetry book. He has recovered from his heart attack and is hospitalized at a cardiovascular recovery clinic. Next to him a young woman caresses his head. It's his daughter, Milona, a student in England.

He feels quiet and broken by all the ordeal that brought him into this situation. He no longer wants to solve any mystery. He wants to live for his children and in particular wants to be healthy to prepare a bright future for them. He will close down all his businesses and retire to a small, quiet country where no one will know about him. He is thinking of settling in the Maldives or Liechtenstein—a country where no one will ever know him.

The nurse approaches his bench and tells him that a gentleman is looking for him. A well-dressed gentleman with a big beard and piercing green eyes is walking toward him. Money starts a bit and stands up. "Hey, how are you doing?"

"Okay, Money. I'm here to see what you're doing."

"How long has it been since I've seen you?"

"At least a decade."

They both smile and embrace.

"Money, what's the deal with David Baldoni?"

"How do you know about him?"

"You forget where I work. He was my workmate at the Agency. He was my pupil."

"Well, I hired him to find some compromising information, to exact revenge on certain people."

"You know that by your deeds you killed Page."

"Is Nick dead?"

"Yes, he betrayed and sold information. The Shadows have taken care of him. Who did you want to avenge?"

"The Black Order, as well as the Katharsis. They didn't get me, on the grounds that I didn't have mystical guidance. Now I know what their mysticism is—intoxication, drugs, and loose women."

"I don't need to tell you that you upset the organization. That's why they sent a sign to you."

"I thought so, and what do I have to do?"

"Send the money to David, get rid of the file he's going to send you in a few days, and go wherever you want. I'll talk to the organization and tell them you're dead."

"And where should I go?"

"Leave for some unknown island. Go to French Polynesia, change your name, and then come back."

"Won't I have some shadow following me?"

"No! I talked to the assassin, and he's not going to do anything. They're only going to send a few murderers for show. You know, I care about you and David. I want to save you. You've got yourself into a big mess."

"Who are you working for?"

"I think you know. For the top of the pyramid."

"I imagined so. Thank you for remaining the same eternally faithful friend."

They link arms and go to another bench, Money leaning heavily on the strong arm of his friend.

"Money, I suspect you still have financial resources?"

"Enough to live for millions of years."

"Then go and enjoy it. When you decide to leave here, send me an email. I'll come and help you change your name and maybe even your appearance."

"I'll go as far as I can, to Oceania."

"That's the best. Just stay there for a while."

"How long?"

"Until I seek you out; then you will know that the organization has forgotten you. I'll see that somehow, in a month or two, some news appears in the press saying that you've died."

"What are you going to do with David?"

"I'll manipulate him until he realizes that he has to give up this plan. I can protect you, but I cannot betray the Organization. Nick, Willie, even Morowitz have betrayed the Golden Law, the *Mystery above everything*. No one in this world needs to know what's in the Mystery. We can talk about anything you want except for that. You know better, Money."

"Thank you for being a truthful friend."

"You know I won't forget your help. When I had nothing to eat, you gave me a good hand."

"But why are you protecting David?"

"Because I care very much about him."

"I know he was your pupil, but you are particularly fond of him."

"I'll tell you a secret that will die only between us. Do you agree?"

"Sure."

"David is my sister Betty's son—the one who died of cancer twenty years ago."

"Are you serious?"

"Yes, he was raised by his father and his grandmother. Then when he finished college, he came into the Agency, and I taught him everything he knows. Afterward I helped him all the time, more or less privately."

"You amaze me. I was sure you had a deep connection with him, but I didn't suspect this."

Money looks at the recovery center building, and his companion looks right at him. He makes a sign known only to them and then walks away across the broad green lawn. Behind them rises the sound of the stirring birds. *The rain is probably coming*, thinks Money, leaving for his room.

earing an angelic choir from afar, Abraham Watson walks faster. He passes stores full of advertisements and cheap products. The closer he gets, the better the choir can be heard. He enters the church, where a *Te Deum* is shaking the building.

White-robed children are singing under the priest's direction. After he makes the ritual signals at the end of the service, he turns back to the choir. After half an hour of singing, they finish, and the people slowly file out.

Watson approaches the altar. The priest notices him and signals him to wait outside. After the priest talks to the parents of the children, they all embrace and emerge from the door.

Watson goes to him and murmurs, "We need to talk urgently."

"Okay, we'll go to my house. Wait a minute for me to lock the church, and then we'll go."

"All right." After the priest makes sure everything is in order, he takes a handful of candles and a book and leaves side by side with Watson. They walk slowly, casually, looking at the sky. The priest doesn't live far from the church, so in less than ten minutes they arrive at his home. They descend to the basement, where the priest has a small bed, an altar, and a library.

Watson looks at the priest's modest furnishings and marvels. "Father, you really live like in the old times."

"You know, Abraham, that I have an everlasting respect for early Christianity."

"Yes, but the world has evolved."

"You're right. What am I going to do? That's me, old-fashioned. Faith goes arm to arm with humility." He gives Watson a stern look. "Tell me what happened."

"Did you know that Nick's been killed? I think David and Wilson are involved."

"That's not true. None of them is involved. Nick gave the wrong order."

"What did the order say?"

"I haven't spoken to them, but I know betrayal is paying dearly. You know just how the organization repays betrayal."

"Yes, the *eyes don't see, the mouth no longer speaks, the ears no longer hear.* It's a death sentence. Why did they kill him?"

"Because he talked about Money."

"How do you know?"

"You forget that I am part of the Order too."

"Indeed. It's hard to imagine, you who are such a good person."

"The Order does not deal with such things, only the Organization. I found out who killed him."

"Who?"

"Vick. He was Nick's shadow. That's why he disappeared."

"Vicktor Stringe. Is he the actual assassin?"

"Yes, Abraham. I see you're extremely surprised."

"I know there was no great friendship between them. But I didn't think so."

"Well, here it was."

"How do you know?"

"I know, but I can't tell you the source."

"Where is Vick now?"

"He disappeared and left me a file to pass to someone."

"To whom?"

"I'm not telling you because it was his last request."

"What does the file say?"

"Some information about him and the organization."

"I bet nobody knows that Vicktor is who he really is."

"Yes, one single person knows: Wilson."

"Well, how does he know?"

"He has a very strong relationship with the Order of Shadows."

"Don't tell me he's part of the Order?"

"Not really, but he's got a lot of knowledge there."

"Father, how does religion and everything you preach go along with the rest of your work?"

"You can't understand. The order was founded to protect the legacy of Christianity. Christianity has mysteries that cannot be touched and known to anyone."

"Right, but you know that the Black Order of the Sacred Seat is highly disputed."

"All that is unknown is questionable. You know this, Abraham."

The priest leans over to Abraham and on a piece of paper he writes a phrase that shakes Abraham. He rises slowly, nods, and leaves. The priest looks at him, smiling calmly. Abraham enjoys not being part of the Agency or any other organization or society.

Outside a small rain begins to pelt the asphalt. The priest's thoughts fly to divine Misericordia and to the souls of the dead that no one will ever remember.

David wakes up full of good cheer with Amy. They hug. He loves this woman very much, a woman who has endured his whims for a long time. She's about to go to work, and he'll be finishing the job he was paid for.

After a long kiss, Amy leaves as if she's floating down the stairs. He closes the door and quickly goes to the computer, where he writes a short email to Vick, a note of gratitude. He comes out of the house with an envelope that he sends to the address given by Money. Then he comes home with the thought of reading Vick's entire file. From the roadside, he buys three big, beautiful lilies for Amy. He sits in the armchair drinking a tea and opens the file. A phone is ringing silently.

"Hello."

"Hi, David, thanks for everything."

"Who is this?"

"Money. I got your email. I'm sure the envelope will arrive. By noon tomorrow you will have all the money in your account. Thanks for your collaboration. Now you can have that quiet life."

"Thank you so much, Money. I'm glad I met you. I hope we meet in this life or maybe in the other one."

"Surely in the other one, David. I assure you."

"Okay, Money, may you stay healthy."

"All the best to you, my friend."

"The same to you." Cheerful, he decides to read Vick's file faster. He opens the file. First he notices some information about each organization and then finds pictures from different meetings. Then there's a small photo album with the leading members of the world's great organizations. He can't believe it; Vick knew all these things, and now he's passed it all to him. Row by row are short names of famous people, ministers, heads of state, cardinals, bishops, bankers, businessmen, actors, musicians, athletes, princes, and kings. All the world's elite are in these organizations.

The last item in the envelope is a black envelope with a strange badge: a mask surrounded by concentric circles, full of esoteric symbolism. He opens the envelope to find an empty sheet that says: "*I am the ORGANIZATION. Now that you've found out, forget it ALL.*"

He doesn't understand the exact message. He's looking through the whole file again. He observes the same information, documents, official lists, and offices of various secret and discreet societies. On the back of the black envelope he notes written in block letters, in golden ink: "The *power* is *in the hands* of those who *do not know* that they hold it."

He throws the envelope on the floor in anger. *Vick betrayed me by not telling me the whole truth*, David is thinking. He reassembles the whole file and slides it under the bed.

At the door Amy calls, anxious to come in. "Hi, David. I have a surprise for you."

"What?"

"I want us to leave for a month in the exotic islands, just the two of us. I have two tickets to paradise, one way only."

"That's what I was going to do myself. I'll take a look and book to stay for more than a month."

"But you know we have to think about money, too," Amy adds.

"Stay calm; everything is solved. We have money to stay there all our lives. Don't forget, I sold the detective company."

"Okay, if you say so. I hope you didn't get into trouble."

"None of that; it's all over." He hugs her, and they rush like two young lovers to the bedroom. After hours of passion they both fall asleep exhausted.

David wakes up to drink some water and looks to the file. Then secretly, because he had promised Amy that he would stay off his computer for a year, he opens his email and notices his inbox is full. He reads the messages and deletes them all. But as he clicks *delete* at the last one, he notices a strange address. He looks in the trash folder and reads where he got the mail from: MasterofShadow1@gmail.com. He opens it and reads a short text.

> David, you don't know who I am and you don't even have to. I'm a friend who protects you. You've learned too much. Please destroy the file you own, forget all the information, and go somewhere else. I can't protect you for long.
> A friend of yours.

He turns off his computer and goes fast to the bedroom next to Amy. Tomorrow he'll explain to her that he is certain he wants to live with her in a paradise where there are no concerns or other problems. He caresses her hair and tries to fall asleep. Thoughts don't leave him alone; he's struggling, anxious. Something urges him to find out what that envelope or message means. How can he find out ... what is the truth? He can hardly sleep.

XIV

David wakes up in a ghost town. He doesn't know how he got here. All the buildings are deserted. Horrified, he walks until he finds a door at a store. He opens it, and there in the moonlight he notices many carnival costumes, masks, and disguises. He goes to each one and looks closely. All these seem so vivid that he shudders at the possibility that these costumes have a life of their own.

On the counter in front of him is written in big letters, *Welcome to the world of lies. If you're one of ours, wear a costume, or put on a mask.* He comes out of the store terrified and arrives in a cinema. There's a movie running. The seats are empty, there is no one in the audience. The film shows images of people's lives. The main character is an ordinary man who is fooled at every step by someone else. Above them a huge hand guides them through what to do. The character repeats almost obsessively the same phrase, "How do I get rid of this lie? Freedom is a lie of history."

Coming out of the cinema, he heads toward the city center. There all the people sit with their eyes looking at a fixed point. A large screen displays the benefits of the modern world and freedom. People are promised heavenly happiness. Behind them on bleachers, people with masks discuss and laugh loudly at those who look fascinated at the screen.

He leaves the town on foot. Along the way, he notices a black wind moving toward the city and a red wind leaving the city. After the same two images he hears warrior cries; a battle has broken out in the city. He reaches the next town but can't get in. He has to pay a huge fee, and he has no money. It's the city of well-being. Then he heads toward a wooden city, where poor people receive him with open arms. He enters this city and notices that even though people have nothing to eat, they share everything with him.

He quickly comes out and goes to a village where tall and solid people stay melancholic and look at each other. Then he heads to a valley on which the word *power* is written. From the valley someone calls his name: *David, David, David.*

"David, wake up. We have to pack. Aren't we leaving today?"

"Yes, we are. I'm sorry; I had a very interesting dream."

"What exactly did you dream about?"

"I think the truth, Amy. I'm not sure, but I think I know."

"Okay, I'm going to go buy some items. Will you come with me?"

"No, I'm going to solve another problem, and then I'll pack my bags."

They kiss passionately, and Amy leaves. Then David goes into the kitchen and has a cup of coffee. He's watching celebrity news on TV. Then, pondering, he's looking at the file again. On the black envelope he notices the coat of arms and ... That's it! He remembers it as the coat of the ghost city.

He picks up the phone and calls a friend. After a few rings he responds.

"Jimmy, I want to ask you something important. Please, this is a favor for which I will not have enough years to thank you, I'm aware. But I beg you to help me."

"All right. You know we're friends. Say it, David."

"Can you publish a letter to someone on a page tomorrow?"

"What's this about?"

"It's a letter of a friend to humankind. It's a warning he sent me before he died. Please."

"Okay, I'll publish it. But what does it contain?"

"Information about a global secret society."

"It's risky, but you know there's no censorship in me. Was it signed or not?"

"Not. It will appear with a pseudonym."

"Okay, send it today."

"Within the hour. I have something else to take care of."

"Well, I'm waiting. By the way, how are you?"

"I'm getting married and going on a long honeymoon. I'll be back eventually."

"Well, I'll wait for you for a coffee when you get back. I want you to collaborate on the paper or the new magazine."

"It will be my pleasure, Jimmy. I think we'll talk next year."

"Good. All the best, and have a fantastic honeymoon."

"Thanks, Jimmy, you're a true friend."

XV

David turns on his computer and takes his coffee cup. He lights one last cigarette, deciding never to smoke again. He closes all the windows and doors. He calls Amy, who by luck has met her best friend, and they're going to engage in girls' gossip for a couple of hours. He looks at the note. He's got eight hours before they go on a cruise. He opens a document in Word, takes a deep breath, and starts typing.

Letter to Humankind:

History has always fascinated the people who live on this earth. History has been built of facts, exceptional people, and unique happenings. Everything that represents history is a mystification of truth. The forces that ruled history have always remained unknown to nearly everyone. I confess that I thought the world was run by secret and discreet societies. I was mistaken.

The world is ruled by a cabal of powerful men. The world's supreme elite is part of an organization. The organization is called the MASK. The organization does not have a precise headquarters or a leading group. It is driven by passion and by people's desire to overthrow the hierarchies in the world.

People are weak beings fascinated by power. Everyone is outraged that the sea or the mountain is stronger than they. People are outraged that God or the devil is stronger than them. That's why people invented secret and discreet organizations, to govern and master other people. This is a fulfillment of the ambition of human nature. It is a revenge of human nature against the stand-alone nature. It's the last slave uprising. It is the riot of physical history against metaphysical history.

Legendarily, the world is ruled by three eternal wise people: Rotham the Black, Gahael, and Elihaim, who are the alter egos of the angels of God. In short, they are souls who have risen against God and are cursed forever. They are not demons; they are wizards who have played with the forces that govern the universe. They are subordinated to several groups, such as the Group of the Thirteen Judges, the World Business Club, the World Economic Club, the Planetary Industrial Group, the Katharsis Organization, and the Black Order of the Sacred Seat. All these societies are helped by strong, criminal groups, and Intelligence Services. Their ultimate goal is to lead and enslave the world. Why? Because it is the commandment of evil that lies in each of us.

The MASK organization is the generic name for the members of these societies who work for the enslavement of humankind. They fulfill these provisions with masks on their face and souls hidden from everyone. The great reality of this organization is that even those who are part of it do not realize that they are involved. It's a generic name I found after a long search. It is a definition of the treachery of Iscariot, a deception of God's creation. I write this letter to warn the world that everything it knows can be untrue or at most mystified.

With deepest good wishes, a mere friend of humankind.

David finishes and leans back, exhausted. A great weight disappears from his shoulders. He sends an email to Jimmy, who confirms that he has received it and will publish it tomorrow. David takes the green file and tears it into small pieces, including all the pictures. He throws everything in the trash. There, a neighbor asks him what all those pieces of paper are. He answers that they are memories from another life.

Then he calls the block manager and pays him every charge for the entire next year. Finally, he packs and waits for Amy. Tomorrow, when everything appears in the paper, he will be far away and will forget everything. He doesn't want to know what happens to the others.

He dresses quickly and goes to the bank to check the account. He is shocked. There is a deposit of tens of millions of euros in his account. *Mr. Money was extremely generous,* David thinks. He withdraws a significant amount and transfers his account to another bank in a tax haven, with the help of a banker friend. He makes sure no one will know what accounts he owns.

Full of hope, he returns home. At the curb a black car with tinted windows awaits him. He freezes with fear, thinking that all of his plans can be destroyed instantly. Wilson emerges from the car and hugs him.

"David, I hope you gave up everything."

"Yes, I sent Money the 'Planet' file, and I'm leaving with Amy."

"Go away as far as you can, and stay as long as possible."

"I was going to go on an island, somewhere."

"Do you need anything?"

"No, Money ensured my future," and for the first time he laughs loudly.

"That's very good," Wilson says, smiling.

"Wilson, now at the end, you know what was behind all this matter?"

"No, but if I knew, I'd tell you. An eccentric guy wanted to find secrets bigger than his hat. But why are you asking me?"

"Sometimes I feel like you know a lot more."

"Ah, bollocks. You know I retired. By the way, don't freak out; this is the car that will take you and your luggage all the way to the cruise. You think, even if I retired, I don't still have a little pull here and there?"

"Yes, quite seriously!"

The two hug again, and Wilson gives him a golden necklace. David asks him what this chain is for. He tells him he has to keep it for luck. In the distance he sees Amy returning happily. Wilson sets off on foot, and David waits for Amy. They will leave together from this miserable life, David thinks happily.

XVI

I n a large anteroom full of dark light, they are invited to sit down and offered coffee. Wilson is thinking about why he was called by the director of the Agency. He hasn't spoken to him for years. All around him, young people are bustling with files and tapping on laptops. Happy and enthusiastic, they do not feel fatigue. Wilson smiles, thinking about his own youth.

A tall man calls him. "Mr. Smith, you are expected."

Wilson rises and heads toward the big wooden door. He enters the room and notices an enormous desk flanked by two bookshelves as large as the wall. On a black leather chair a middle-aged man with glasses and black hair reads a file.

"Please have a seat."

"Thank you, Director."

"You can call me Edward. We've known each other for a long time, Wilson."

"Certainly. Why did you call me?"

"How long has it been since you were in this office last time?"

"I don't know. It's been a while."

"I took over the Agency more than ten years ago. You were my coworker and my friend. You were always in charge of the Agency whenever I wasn't here. Tell me, why you didn't tell me anything about this case?"

"Eddie, I think you know better. Money hired my nephew to find out everything. And I wanted to protect him."

"I agree, but you know he's learned a lot of secret things."

"Where's Nick?"

"I don't know, Wilson, I'm telling you honestly."

"What about Vick?"

"What I do know is that Vick lives somewhere in Northern Europe—if I'm not mistaken, in Norway. Before he left, I saw him. He confessed everything."

"I was sure, but what you don't know is that Vick is a shadow."

"How do you know?"

"You forget that that's why you got me involved; I have a few contacts. Why did you call me?"

"To make sure the Agency is not involved."

"Not a bit. The Agency is not even mentioned in this file. Are you aware that David knows everything?"

"Yes, I know, but I also know that you're defending him and that you're going to send him somewhere."

"Indeed, Eddie."

"But Money—what's his role?"

"He was the protégé of everyone. He gave money here and there. But now he's sick, he's retired."

"Good to see you. In your presence I'm closing the case, I'm going to order no one to investigate anything. Look, I'm destroying the file, but I want you to promise me something: that what David found out about the Agency, nobody will ever find out. Otherwise he can talk about whatever he wants; I don't care."

"Of course, Eddie. You know I keep my word."

"Thanks."

The two men rise from their chairs and hug. The director shows Wilson the office, talking about their predecessors. Wilson thanks him and tells him he has to visit his farm.

As he grasps the doorknob, the director says: "Wilson, I know everything, I have microphones everywhere. And I know you're the big shadow."

"I knew you know, Eddie. I also knew that you were one of my trusted friends."

The two look eye to eye, and Wilson leaves. The director sits down and makes a short phone call. Wilson walks out of the building, gets into his car, and turns on the radio, which is set on country music. A big smile illuminates his face.

EPILOGUE

David jumps in the water and swims under the hot sun rays Amy is on the yacht; she calls him to come quick to read some news. He jumps out wet as he is and slides on the deck, hitting his hand, but he is cheerful because he is in paradise with the woman he has always loved.

In the newspaper there is more news about failing banks and the financial and economic crisis. But a back page story relates that the billionaire Sergei Alexandrovich Mill, nicknamed Money, had a fatal heart attack in Moscow. David thinks about him and looks to heaven. He knows that Money smiles at them from up there.

In a crowded, smoky café, Wilson swears angrily. The bastard had the guts to write. If it wasn't for my nephew, it had been over for a long time. It was the secret, well-known; now, bastards, everyone knows who you are. And his noisy laugh rings through the café.

Amy tells him that a letter was published in a famous newspaper that rocked the world. David assures her that it is an invention to provide publicity and better sell the newspaper. They look to the water, and the emerald reflections remind him of the mystery behind anything that has the color of the grass. Nature is green and is full of mysteries.

David smiles. "Mystery above all," he cries out to Amy, who throws herself into the warm, crystal-clear water of an exotic sea.

He plunges in beside her and says, "Amy, I want us to live here for the rest of our lives, and believe me, we can afford it. An angel has taken care of us." David raises both hands to the clear sky.

Amy shakes her head to indicate she doesn't understand and then twirls a finger beside her head, saying he's crazy. She emerges from the water and lies on the lounger, arranging her body in an ideal position for tanning. She is happy now, truly happy because she is now living a good life for real. She looks at David, who is swimming cheerfully near the multicolored fishes.

Far away, on another sea, a soul lives in a quiet that he has not had for a long time. A silence before the passage to the other side.

David returns to the yacht, where he sees Amy is asleep. He reclines at her side, takes her hand, and looks at the sun, which seems to be smiling at him. He also looks at the sky, which goes silent forever although it is aware of his mystery.

Printed in the United States
by Baker & Taylor Publisher Services